Lerner SPORTS™

I0866934

SPORTS ALL-STARS

AARON DONALD

Lerner Publications Company
An imprint of Lerner Publishing Group, Inc.
241 First Avenue North
Minneapolis, MN 55401 USA

For reading levels and more information, look up this title at www.lernerbooks.com.

Main body text set in Albany Std. Typeface provided by Agfa.

Library of Congress Cataloging-in-Publication Data

Names: Hill, Christina, author.
Title: Aaron Donald / Christina Hill.
Description: Minneapolis : Lerner Publications, [2022] | Series: Sports all-stars (Lerner sports) | Includes bibliographical references and index. | Audience: Ages 7–11 | Audience: Grades 2–3 | Summary: "Aaron Donald's size, speed, and strength make him one of the toughest defensive linemen in football. See how the Los Angeles Rams player reached the NFL, what he does to stay strong, and much more"— Provided by publisher.
Identifiers: LCCN 2021035989 (print) | LCCN 2021035990 (ebook) | ISBN 9781728441207 (library binding) | ISBN 9781728449432 (paperback) | ISBN 9781728445168 (ebook)
Subjects: LCSH: Donald, Aaron, 1991—-Juvenile literature. | Los Angeles Rams (Football team : 2016-)—Juvenile literature. | Line play (Football)—Juvenile literature. | Football players—United States—Biography—Juvenile literature.
Classification: LCC GV939.D646 H55 2022 (print) | LCC GV939.D646 (ebook) | DDC 796.33092 [B]—dc23

LC record available at https://lccn.loc.gov/2021035989
LC ebook record available at https://lccn.loc.gov/2021035990

Manufactured in the United States of America
1-49891-49734-7/15/2021

TABLE OF CONTENTS

FOUR-SACK GAME

Aaron Donald celebrates a good play against the San Francisco 49ers in 2018.

The Los Angeles Rams were playing the San Francisco 49ers on October 21, 2018. The Rams were one of the best scoring teams in the National Football League (NFL). But on that day, the Rams defense completely dominated the game.

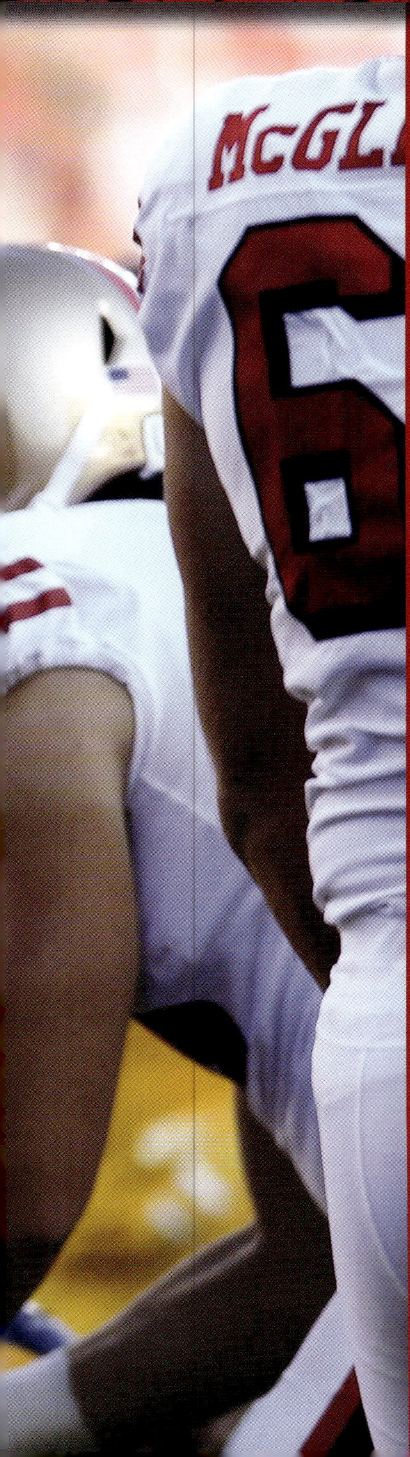

FACTS AT A GLANCE

- **Date of birth:** May 23, 1991
- **Position:** defensive tackle
- **League:** NFL
- **Professional highlights:** set a record for the fastest 40-yard dash time (4.68 seconds) for a defensive tackle; named Defensive Rookie of the Year in 2014; won the NFL Defensive Player of the Year award in 2017, 2018, and 2020
- **Personal highlights:** grew up in Pittsburgh, Pennsylvania; attended the University of Pittsburgh; has two children, Jaeda and Aaron Jr.

Donald (*left*) takes the football from Matt Breida of the 49ers during a tackle.

Defensive tackle Aaron Donald wore number 99 for the Rams. He controlled the middle of the field. His strong plays made it hard for the 49ers to gain yards.

Late in the first quarter, 49ers running back Matt Breida had the ball. Donald tackled him. As the two players were falling to the ground, Donald reached out. With one swift motion, he grabbed the ball out of Breida's hands. The football never touched the ground. Donald managed to force a fumble and recover it all at once.

The Rams beat the 49ers 39–10. The Rams sacked the quarterback seven times. Four of those sacks belonged to Donald.

Donald earned the National Football Conference (NFC) Defensive Player of the Week award after his record-setting game. He went on to become the NFL sacks leader that season with 20.5.

A reporter asked Donald if he ever thought he would have a four-sack game. "You never know what can happen," Donald said. "But I know my daughter wanted me to get ten and my son wanted me to get three, so I hope they're going to be happy with four."

Donald earns more than $22.5 million per season from the Rams. He is the highest-paid defender in the NFL.

FOOTBALL FAMILY

Aaron Donald (left) chases Syracuse quarterback Ryan Nassib during a college game.

Aaron Donald was born on May 23, 1991. He grew up in Pittsburgh, Pennsylvania, with his older brother and sister. His dad, Archie, played football in college. Injuries prevented Archie from reaching the NFL. But he still loved football

Aaron grew up in Pittsburgh, Pennsylvania.

and continued to work out every day. He built a gym in the basement that the family called the "dungeon."

Aaron and his brother, Archie Jr., liked watching their dad lift weights. They were impressed by his strength. When Aaron was 12, his dad said he could start working out with him.

As soon as Aaron saw his own muscles growing, he was hooked. He and his brother spent their teenage years waking up early to lift weights with their dad before school.

"A lot of my success, and a lot of who I am now, is because of my dad, and the way he raised me and taught me how to have a work ethic," Aaron said.

Aaron and his brother both loved playing football, just like their dad did. Aaron played at Penn Hills High School. His talent on the football field made him a high school star.

Donald racked up 29.5 sacks in four seasons at the University of Pittsburgh.

Aaron's senior season at Pittsburgh earned him four major awards, including the Bronko Nagurski Trophy for the nation's most outstanding defensive player.

Donald won many awards during his successful high school career. But the big football colleges overlooked him. He was smaller than most college defensive tackles.

In 2010, the University of Pittsburgh offered Donald a scholarship. He was happy to stay close to home. He worked hard for the Pittsburgh football team. After four years at the school, he was ready for the NFL.

During the 2014 NFL Combine, Donald made a big impression on fans and coaches. The NFL Combine is a place for college players to show off their skills. NFL scouts and coaches watch the players perform strength, speed, and skills tests. Donald ran the 40-yard (37 m)

Donald was joined by Rams head coach Jeff Fischer (*left*) and the team's general manager, Les Snead (*right*), during the 2014 draft.

dash in 4.68 seconds. He also lifted 225 pounds (102 kg) 35 times on the bench press. The Rams were impressed. They chose Donald with the 13th overall pick in the 2014 draft.

SUPERSTRONG AND HUNGRY

Donald warms up on the field before a game against the Minnesota Vikings.

Donald admits that he didn't get enough exercise as a young kid. But when he started lifting weights with his dad, he got bigger and stronger. He could see the results of his hard work.

Donald loves playing football and works hard during practice to improve his skills.

In 2018, Donald signed a contract with the Rams that would pay him $135 million over six years. Donald used some of the money to buy his dad a new house. But he begged his dad to never sell his childhood home. Donald sometimes meets his dad and his brother in the basement gym. They lift weights together in the dungeon, just like they did when they were younger.

Donald is known for his strength and positive attitude.

Donald has extreme strength, which comes from his intense workouts. His workouts include lifting as much as 500 pounds (227 kg) on the bench press. Bench press exercises mainly strengthen an athlete's chest and arm muscles. But Donald also loves to work on strengthening his stomach. He does different kinds of crunches to target all of his stomach muscles.

Donald (*right*) gets the energy he needs to make big plays on the field from his healthful diet.

Donald's workouts burn a lot of energy. To replace that energy, he eats almost 5,000 calories per day. This is almost twice the amount that an average man consumes. Donald's diet is about 50 percent carbohydrates. Carbohydrates are found in foods like pasta and rice. Around 20 percent of his diet is protein from chicken, turkey, or beef. He also consumes a lot of healthy fats from foods like fish and avocados.

Maintaining his weight helps Donald play great defense. If he weighed less, opposing players might be able to push him around on the football field. But he has a busy schedule. Donald found himself losing weight because he didn't have time to cook healthful meals. So he hired Arron Sain to help him. Sain is a personal chef who knows what Donald needs to keep his body fueled for big games.

Donald's favorite food is Sain's breakfast tacos. They're made with eggs, spicy turkey sausage, cheese, and lots of vegetables. Donald loves to eat them before his morning practices. It gives him the energy he needs to work hard.

Donald's chef makes a cheat-day dish called "Dancing Meatballs." The first time Donald ate it, he danced around the kitchen.

BIG GIVER

Donald takes time to pose for photos with fans.

Doug Baldwin played for the Seattle Seahawks from 2011 to 2018.

Donald is generous and is known for his charity work. In 2016, he played the Madden NFL video game in an Xbox Charity Challenge. Donald faced Seattle Seahawks player Doug Baldwin. Donald won the game and earned $51,000 for the Make-A-Wish Foundation. The Make-A-Wish Foundation grants special wishes to children battling illnesses.

"I don't think I've ever had that much fun playing Madden," said Donald. "Doug was a fierce competitor

Heinz Field has been the home of the Pittsburgh Panthers and the Pittsburgh Steelers since 2001.

tonight, but so thankful I was able to pull off a championship win and give back to the Make-A-Wish Foundation."

In 2018, Donald had the chance to make a wish come true for a boy named Colson. Donald called Colson on the phone and gave him tickets to a Rams game. Colson even got to work as the water boy for the team during the game.

Donald's success in the NFL allows him the chance to give back to the people and places that helped him along the way. In 2019, he gave money to the University of Pittsburgh. The gift will be used to improve the team's training facilities. "My experience as a [Pittsburgh] Panther is something that influences my life every day and I want to pay that forward," said Donald.

In 2019, Donald started a new foundation called AD99 Solutions. It helps kids in his hometown of Pittsburgh. Donald grew up playing sports. He wants to make sure other kids have the same chance to play that he had. AD99 Solutions provides safe places for kids to play sports. It also teaches them about healthful eating.

Donald racked up 115 tackles during his time at the University of Pittsburgh.

Donald appeared in a Nike advertisement celebrating sports in 2020.

Donald's success on the football field means that many companies want him to endorse their products. Support from a famous athlete can help businesses boost their sales. Companies often want to work with high-profile players such as quarterbacks instead of defensive tackles. But Donald's popularity with fans has won over many companies. He represents companies such as Pizza Hut, Dick's Sporting Goods, and Karma Automotive.

Ping-Pong Pizza Party

Donald has been playing ping-pong as a hobby since he was 14. He likes to challenge his teammates to play. Donald joined forces with Pizza Hut to share two of his favorite things: pizza and ping-pong. Fans can use their phones to scan their Pizza Hut pizza box and enter a contest. One of the prizes is playing ping-pong with Donald.

Donald began working with Pizza Hut in 2019.

Marianne Radley is a Pizza Hut official. She explained why they chose Donald to endorse their pizza. "Aaron really stood out because of his love of pizza, charismatic personality, and of course, his incredible play on the field," Radley said. "He's just a perfect fit."

BECOMING A STAR

Donald makes a tackle during the 2015 Pro Bowl.

Despite being overlooked early in his career, Donald's dedication to football and his intense training and hard work have paid off. Donald's NFL success started his first year when

Donald was named *Sports Illustrated* Performer of the Year in 2018.

he won the 2014 Defensive Rookie of the Year Award. His skills continue to improve each season.

Donald has been racking up awards and honors. He has been voted into the NFL Pro Bowl seven times. The Pro Bowl is the NFL's all-star game featuring the best players in the league. Donald was named NFC Defensive Player of the Week seven times and Defensive Player of the Month two times.

Donald knocks down quarterback Tom Brady during the 2019 Super Bowl.

Donald is one of the best defensive tackles in NFL history. He won the Defensive Player of the Year Award in 2017, 2018, and 2020. Only two other players have won this award three times. With Donald's help, the Rams had the number-one defense in points scored against them and yards allowed in 2020.

Donald helped the Rams make it to the 2019 Super Bowl. They lost to the New England Patriots, but Donald is determined to win the NFL championship. “I just go out there and play hard because I want to be productive,” Donald said. “I want to win games and I want to get to a certain point where at the end of the year, we can hold up that trophy.”

All-Star Stats

Since Donald joined the NFL in 2014, he has always ranked near the top of the sacks leaderboard. Take a look at where he ranked in 2020 compared to the NFL's other best defensive players.

NFL Sacks Leaders for 2020

Rank	Player	Sacks
1.	T.J. Watt	15.0
2.	Aaron Donald	13.5
3.	Trey Hendrickson	13.5
4.	Haason Reddick	12.5
5.	Za'Darius Smith	12.5
6.	Myles Garrett	12.0
7.	Leonard Williams	11.5
8.	Stephon Tuitt	11.0
9.	Leonard Floyd	10.5
10.	Romeo Okwara	10.0

Glossary

bench press: an exercise in which a weight is raised by extending the arms upward while lying on a bench

carbohydrate: a substance that is rich in energy and is made up of carbon, hydrogen, and oxygen

charismatic: a person who has charm and appeal

crunch: a stomach exercise similar to a sit-up

defensive tackle: a defender in football who plays in the middle of the defensive line

endorse: to recommend something, such as a product or service, usually in exchange for money

fumble: when a football player loses hold of the ball while handling or running with it

protein: a nutrient found in food that is a necessary part of the diet

recruit: to find new players and get them to join a team or other group

sack: to tackle the quarterback for a loss of yards

scholarship: money that a school or another group gives to students to help pay for their education

scout: a person who judges the skills of athletes

Source Notes

7 Cameron DaSilva, "Aaron Donald Has 'Room for Improvement' after 4-Sack Game vs. 49ers," October 22, 2018, https://theramswire.usatoday.com/2018/10/22/nfl-rams-49ers-aaron-donald-sacks-improvement-week-7/.

10 Alden Gonzalez, "How Rams DT Aaron Donald Became the NFL's Most Unstoppable Force," February 2, 2019, https://www.espn.com/blog/nflnation/post/_/id/292361/how-rams-dt-aaron-donald-became-the-nfls-most-unstoppable-force-2.

19 Bryan Kalbrosky, "Aaron Donald Won $51K for Make a Wish Foundation in Madden Tournament," December 7, 2016, https://theramswire.usatoday.com/2016/12/07/los-angeles-rams-aaron-donald-xbox-charity-challenge-make-a-wish/.

21 Luke Torrance, "Aaron Donald Makes 'Historic' 7-Figure Financial Donation to Pitt Football" April 12, 2019, https://www.bizjournals.com/pittsburgh/news/2019/04/12/aaron-donald-makes-historic-7-figure-financial.html.

23 Kristi Dosh, "Pizza Hut Unveils New Ad Campaign For NFL Season," September 10, 2019, https://www.forbes.com/sites/kristidosh/2019/09/10/pizza-hut-unveils-new-ad-campaign-for-nfl-season/?sh=73f619d57864.

27 Eric D. Williams, "Aaron Donald Wins Third NFL Defensive Player of the Year Award," February 6, 2021, https://www.si.com/nfl/rams/news/la-rams-dt-aaron-donald-wins-third-defensive-player-of-year-award.

Learn More

AD99 Solutions
https://ad99.org/

Los Angeles Rams
https://www.therams.com

Meier, William. *Los Angeles Rams.* Minneapolis: Abdo, 2020.

Monson, James. *Behind the Scenes Football.* Minneapolis: Lerner Publications, 2020.

NFL
https://www.nfl.com

Patrick, Lee. *Aaron Donald: Football Star.* Lake Elmo, MN: Focus Readers, 2020.

Index

Photo Acknowledgments

Thearon W. Henderson/Stringer/Getty Images, p.4; Thearon W. Henderson/Stringer/Getty Images, p.6; Alan Schwartz/Cal Sport Media/Newscom, p.8; Ken Redding/Getty Images, p.9; Jeanine Leech/Icon SMI/Newscom, p.10; Dilip Vishwanat/Stringer/Getty Images, p.12; Hannah Foslien/Stringer/Getty Images, p.13; Dylan Buell/Stringer/Getty Images, p.14; Alika Jenner/Stringer/Getty Images, p.15; Greg Fiume/Stringer/Getty Images, p.16; Medianews Group/Pasadena Star-Ne/Newscom, p.18; Ralph Freso/Stringer/Getty Images, p.19; Steven W. Adams/Wikimedia, p.20; Image of Sport/Newscom, p.22; Carlos Becerra/Stringer/Getty Images, p.23; Christian Petersen/Staff/Getty Images, p.24; Rich Polk / Stringer/Getty Images, p.25; Harry How/Staff/Getty Images, p.26

Cover: Andy Lewis/Icon Sportswire DHW